SPACE AND SILENCE

A COLLECTION OF FLASH FICTION AND ESSAYS

SHUBORNO CHAKROBORTY

Made with ♥ on the Notion Press Platform
www.notionpress.com

To the moments that shaped me—the quiet revelations, the unexpected detours, and the fleeting encounters. For every joy, challenge, and wonder that wove themselves into my life, thank you for giving me stories to tell.

Contents

Contents

Preface

Flash fiction is a very short form of storytelling, typically ranging from a few words to around one thousand words, though some definitions go up to fifteen hundred. The goal is to tell a complete story with a clear narrative arc—usually including a beginning, middle, and end—in a very limited space. Because of its brevity, flash fiction often focuses on a single moment, scene, or character, leaving much to the reader's imagination. Flash fiction is often used to experiment with style and form or to capture moments of deep insight in just a few sentences.

My journey into writing flash fiction began about two years ago in quite an unexpected manner. My nephew, who was nine years old at the time, would request me to tell him a story every night. While crafting stories spontaneously, I observed his reactions. When the stories had unpredictable endings and sudden twists, his eyes would light up. I also noticed that when the stories were half-baked, leaving much to his imagination, he would enter a zone of possibilities. Those storytelling sessions left an indelible mark on me. The idea of leaving the reader with questions and uncertainties seemed like a great way to capture interest and spark the imagination.

Around that time, I moved to IIT Delhi to pursue a master's in public policy. My two years of experience on campus, along with many interactions with people there, gave me a proper boost to write more. The ever-reducing attention span of the general reader was another motivating factor for me. The fundamental aim was to capture that attention span with minimal resources and maximum surprise. Not everyone has the patience to read a never-ending story, which can create a significant cognitive load on the reader. Flash fiction can be seen as an effective tool to reduce that cognitive load while breaking the pattern of monotonous thought processes with a touch of entertainment.

From a writer's perspective, I can also say that writing flash fiction serves as an excellent exercise in creative writing. There are stories all around us. Go to a marketplace, a railway station, or simply sit down in the middle of a university campus with an open mind, and you will find thousands of stories weaving around you. We just need to ask the "what ifs," add a splash of imagination, and a story will emerge.

In this book, I have also included some of my essays, which are more or less structured versions of my opinions and viewpoints about life, society, and its myriad complexities. These opinions are entirely my own and are subject to change with further experiences in my life.

As a self-published author, I often think about making my craft error-free. Getting editors, copyeditors, and proofreaders can be a tough task. So, I have used a combination of QuillBot, Grammarly, and ChatGPT 4.0. For copyediting and proofreading, I used the prompt: "Act like a copyeditor and proofreader and edit this chapter according to the Chicago Manual of Style. Focus on punctuation, grammar, syntax, typos, capitalization, formatting, and consistency. Format all numbers according to the Chicago Manual of Style, spelling them out if necessary. Hyphenate double adjectives before a noun. If a single word has been split into two words, combine it into a single word." This prompt claims to remove up to 94% of errors, so I trusted it and used it to proofread and copyedit the chapters in this book.

Acknowledgements

To my loving family, especially my elder brother, Mr Shubham Chakroborty, you have remained by my side, through my highs and lows, offering solace during the moments of doubt and celebrating every milestone with unbridled joy. Your unwavering faith in my abilities has fueled my determination to pursue my dreams and push the boundaries of my creativity.

To my teachers in Indian Institute of Technology (IIT) Delhi for enlightening me regarding the intricate connection between technology and society; A special thanks to Centre for Behavioral and Cognitive Sciences (CBCS) Allahabad, for instilling the never ending enthusiasm for understanding the human mind. My four years spent in both these institutes of excellence and eminence have given me a new direction to showcase my creativity and storytelling prowess.

To my experiences, you have been the reason behind the highs and lows in my life. Your majestic way of testing my limits through the fire of emotional turmoil and seemingly hopeless situations has helped me make a comeback each time with greater wisdom and learning than before. I eagerly await more such trials.

To my emotional vulnerabilities, to my impulsivities, to my overthinking mind, to my fickle-mindedness, to my unconventional career, to my loneliness, to my mood swings and most importantly, to my genes. This book wouldn't have been possible without the perfect balance of all these. These are sources behind this creative madness.

Flash Fiction

CHAPTER ONE

THE DICTATOR

In the middle of the city, a man sat at the busiest crossing in a meditative posture. Silence throbbed in the heart of the city. He opened his eyes to find doves sitting around him, with one bird perched on his head. He smiled, finally at peace. He stood up, stretched out his hand, and walked away from the debris of the city he had created after declaring war. No life was left in those once-busy streets anymore, only him—the dictator who wanted to rule everyone but himself.

CHAPTER TWO

THE STORM

"Darling," he said, looking at the deep-blue sky with the sun shining brightly, "this year was no less than a storm." He remarked this with a deep sigh, seemingly unresponsive to the freezing-cold weather. The whirlwind of emotions and turbulent vulnerability made him indifferent to what humanity was seeking, dying for—the elixir of life: love. The stoic emerged by cutting off all ties, embracing uncertainty and equanimity with delight.

CHAPTER THREE

THE COLLATERAL DAMAGE

Two kings were left alone on the battlefield after all the destruction. The war was uncalled for; it was waged just to settle the ego tussles they had once. They remained quiet for a while, looking at the damage their internal world had inflicted on the external world. They could hear the cries all around; their consciences were screaming in agony and pain, yet they were trying to justify it. The collateral damage wasn't collateral anymore. The price of this war was too great to bear. Neither of them left the battlefield—they had nowhere to go. Initially, they thought of a hand-to-hand fight to decide the winner, but they were too tired even for that. They decided to commit suicide. The cyanides in their pockets were waiting for a chance to kill their owners. On the count of three... two... one, they both chewed the capsules simultaneously and waited. Interestingly, neither of them died; both remained alive. Their strategy to see the other dead had failed miserably, as had their integrity, morality, and ethics.

CHAPTER FOUR

The Cat and The Leaf

A cat and a leaf were sunbathing atop a tent. The cat purred contentedly, basking in the warm sun rays that caressed its body, while the leaf, having reached the end of its life cycle, had fallen from a tree adjacent to the tent. The leaf struggled to breathe, wheezing with excruciating pain, while the other leaves could only watch in horror, glimpsing their own eventual fate. Meanwhile, the cat was startled, petrified by the wheezing sound emanating from the dying leaf. Sensing danger, the cat moved to the left, but suddenly tumbled off the tent, caught off guard by an unexpected gust of wind. The force of the wind propelled the leaf, causing both the cat and the leaf to plummet to the ground. As they landed, the leaf fell onto the cat's stomach. The wheezing ceased, and silence enveloped the scene—the leaf no longer struggling, the cat no longer purring.

CHAPTER FIVE

THE GOD'S WILL

"God's will," said the clergyman to the scientist, who had recently lost his daughter in a car accident. The scientist was an atheist. He never agreed without reason or evidence. His life was an inspiration for several upcoming generations. And here he was, standing at the cemetery, listening to the priest and trying to console his heart, which was lagging far behind his rational mind.

"Your god seems to have no emotion," said the scientist with a subtle tone of sarcasm.

"No, He is ever kind, humble, and generous," said the clergyman, not noticing the arrow of sarcasm aimed at him.

"Oh really! Then He could have stopped that scumbag from running his truck over my daughter," said the scientist with a choked voice, trying to control his anger.

The people around him were quiet. The clergyman went silent; he had no answer to console a grieving father.

"Your god isn't humble and kind. Either your perception of God is clouded—in which case, I don't need such a god—or He doesn't exist, and all of you are brainwashed fools," said the scientist, and left the place. Nobody stopped him, not even the rest of his family. The grieving father's wrenching heart had lost the game to his mind.

CHAPTER SIX

THE TUG OF WAR

"Imperfection and impermanence—two words that we must acknowledge daily—subtly define the world we live in. Every tangible and intangible thing around us is both transient and imperfect by nature. Yet, even after we remind ourselves of this, we still seek happiness in things that aren't meant to last forever. Our control over our inner world largely depends on how much we can internalize and realize this concept. But this control leads to resistance, a tug-of-war between the mind and the heart. The heart seeks to break boundaries, while the mind sets them. The heart sees no repercussions, while the mind calculates the risks. Despite this, the heart emerges as the winner, embracing pain and adversity, while the mind retreats into a corner, orchestrating a solitary existence," observed the soul, who was witnessing the intense fight between the mind and the heart of a man returning home after filing for divorce from his wife, who had cheated on him. The mind wanted revenge, while the heart wanted to forgive. The dilemma continued, but the soul remained unfazed by it all.

CHAPTER SEVEN

THE CLOSURE

"I kept detangling the myriad connections of life. With every knot, the network of uncertainties became more complex. The anticipated closure kept becoming more dramatic, yet I struggled to get things done in my own way, trying to achieve full agency over events I never endorsed. The dots, which had seemed connected earlier, revealed the mighty truth of life. There was nothing left to conceal. The truth stood naked, undiluted, and undisputed before me. The chaos turned to silence. The search for closure in flesh and blood gradually washed away, leaving a void. The entire ecosystem provided what I sought. A query arose: Now what next? I was awestruck by the strangeness of my being—incomplete yet complete. The destination had been reached. No more looking back. I have arrived. Let's finally call it a day," wrote the man suffering from a personality disorder in a diary he never knew existed.

CHAPTER EIGHT

THE FIGMENT

The rain fell incessantly, thunderbolts piercing the trees in every direction. He ran madly through the jungle, desperately trying to find his way out. The runner sensed someone trailing behind, attempting to take his life. The freezing-cold night stiffened his joints as spine-chilling raindrops penetrated his torn jacket's collar, which had been ripped by something with big claws that pursued him. He knew one thing: deep within the forest lay an ancient palace where he believed his life would be spared.

After hours of frantic running, he finally caught sight of the palace. Hastily, he opened the main door, which was covered in cobwebs. The ancient lock hung from the latch. Upon entering, he spotted an antique desk and chair occupied by a man writing something. A glimmer of hope arose within him, yet he felt anxious as he cautiously approached, reaching out to tap the man's shoulder. When the man turned around, the runner was bewildered to see himself smiling back—an imagination within his own story. He himself was merely a figment of his own imagination.

CHAPTER NINE

THE PRISON

I looked around in disbelief, finding myself standing in an infinite hall with nothing in sight. It was completely white, lacking any discernible end. Initially, I believed I was confined within a room with white walls, ceiling, and floor. However, when I reached out to touch the walls, I encountered nothing—just an endless void stretching in all directions. The only sensation I experienced was the cold, utterly smooth floor beneath my feet, its color seamlessly blending with the surrounding white. I realized I was stranded in a uniformly homogeneous, boundless space.

As I walked, each pause provided no sense of distance covered—it all appeared identical no matter which way I went. Engrossed in this perplexing environment, I failed to notice my own state—I was devoid of clothes, hair, and even eyebrows. My eyelids were absent too. I found myself trapped in this strange place, sensing a simulated existence, a completely blank canvas with no discernible escape. It was a space without time, lacking detectable edges. My anxiety soared; I screamed, but there was no sound. The question lingered: Why was I there? Who confined me to this infinite prison with no escape?

CHAPTER TEN

THE TRANSITION

The blue skies gradually passed the baton to darkness as mustard-colored lights illuminated the streets. The trees sighed after a long day of dry waves of heat and dust. People rushed back frantically after another day of intense frustration at their workplaces. Their internal chaos transferred to their surroundings through their vehicles. But this cacophony wasn't intense enough to deter two individuals who sat under the tree, staring aimlessly at the traffic while talking to each other about love, life, and existence.

"Do you know, Steve, I love watching the evening sky? The way the shades of blue change makes me think about the life I've had," said Megan, a peaceful smile on her lips.

"Yes, nobody can stop these transitions. It's natural, like how we grow old. Nobody has the power to reverse or change these universal phenomena. It's better to accept it if you can't change it. Life is like a preprogrammed machine, and we are nothing but puppets with no agency," said Steve, looking at the tree where they both used to stay after their untimely demise in a car accident on the road in front of the tree.

After years of troubling passersby with ghostly spells or scaring the life out of people sitting under the tree in the evening, they finally accepted their fate and prepared for the transition to another life, another body, for one more chance to participate in the game of universal puppetry.

CHAPTER ELEVEN

THE FREEDOM TRAP

After years of trial and error, a bird was born. The healthy birdlet became the apple of the eye for every nest holder in the nearby tree. They would flock around to get a glimpse of the newborn. One day, the parents decided to name her. They consulted the entire community of bird-beings to suggest a name. The old bald eagle, the leader of the community, gave her the name "Freedom."

Freedom grew to be a chivalrous, joyful bird who would float around the sky. Her friends enjoyed her company. She would tease the neighbors with her naughty charm. Nobody would utter a single word, but over time, the neighbors grew a little unhappy with the young birdy pie. She would pick fights with the teachers who were teaching her how to fly, but her friends supported her for her unabashed spirit and her ability to call a spade a spade.

Her parents became a little worried, as she would never listen to them. Her rebellious nature started working against her. One day, she would fly with her friends to reach the clouds; the next day, she would reach the depths of the canyon to test her limits. She would never take any advice.

One day, some of her frenemies decided to take her to the depths of the jungle. Her near and dear ones warned her, but to no avail. As she reached the middle of the dense forest, her frenemies left her alone. She lost her sense of direction, cried her heart out, but nobody came forward to help her in the forest full of snakes and spiders. Her claustrophobia made her lose breath, and she collapsed in her own arrogance.

The trees were indifferent, the snakes were hungry, and the wolves fought among themselves for the feast lying unconscious and unfettered. The snakes came first, picked her up, and tore her into pieces. She became the victim of the freedom trap.

CHAPTER TWELVE

THE PONY, THE SNOW AND THE RIDER

I trekked with all my strength, life presenting its challenges directly through my body. Every weary inch of my being cried out in excruciating pain. I reached a point where I wanted to halt, panting heavily, the sweat causing chills. Pondering how the villagers managed that route, I suddenly heard a tinkling sound nearby. Startled, I spotted a pony adorned with a bell around its neck, effortlessly ascending. It glanced at me, then continued onward, pausing briefly to survey the surroundings. Initially skeptical, I sensed the pony needed a rider. Despite lacking experience in pony riding, I settled into the saddle. Slowly, the pony ascended the hill in the biting cold, the altitude making the weather increasingly freezing.

After a grueling three-hour trek, we finally reached the summit, greeted by falling snow. As I gazed at the sky, witnessing snow for the first time, its cottony texture welcomed and embraced us. The joy of completing this challenging trek uplifted me. The pony, too, observed the sky and began braying in delight. Seated on the snow, I relished the freezing weather, the snowfall, and the melodious sound of the pony. It's all about one's perception of the environment. That's what truly matters—your outlook and attitude toward a situation. I sensed this deeply within me. The pain persisted, but it couldn't dominate my mind.

CHAPTER THIRTEEN

THE LAND OF GODS

He cherished collecting an array of pebbles, favoring steel-gray, matte-black, or even the skirmish-red ones. In recent years, his mountain visits had gradually increased. The satisfaction of contributing to the development of remote villages in Uttarakhand was a driving force for him. But beyond that, Uttarakhand—the land of gods, with the eternal Shiva dancing throughout the cosmos—constantly beckoned him.

One fine day in Karnaprayag, at the confluence of the Alaknanda and Pindari rivers, he arrived at the riverbank, where pebbles of all sizes were strewn about. The serene murmur of the river's current induced a natural meditative state in the surroundings. Settling on a large stone, he closed his eyes and immersed himself in the wondrous enigma of life. A fleeting sensation swept over him, as he perceived the river's murmur as the lament of pebbles unwilling to leave their abode for some unknown destination. They had meditated there for ages, sometimes journeying with the rivers to transcend the boundaries of life and death.

He saw Shiva's presence in every pebble, in every minuscule grain of the universe. It was then, for the first time, that he comprehended the vastness of the omnipresent, omniscient, all-pervading energy. Tears welled up in his eyes; he couldn't have asked for more. He had finally unveiled his profound connection with the mountains and the purpose of his life.

CHAPTER FOURTEEN

THE ARCHER

I knew he was my younger brother; skill-wise, I was better than him. One arrow of mine could have cut his head, but I chose not to. Everyone hated me for siding with darkness, for being with the one who chose deceit and treachery. But who will make the world understand that when everybody abandoned me for being part of the downtrodden, he was the one who gave me my due? His friendship restored my lost respect. I knew he was wrong, a sinner, but how could I be disloyal to him?

My other younger brothers were dear to me, yet they despised me. Still, I secretly loved them to protect our mother's dignity. I even donated my protection, my shield, to the disguised demigod, never letting anyone go empty-handed. Yet, even after many years, centuries, and millennia, people remember me as a traitor, as a sinner. Nobody understood my predicament. They built a temple for me, named a region after me, but nobody comes to see me, to understand and experience my loneliness.

I might serve as a bad example, the antithesis of Arjuna, the greatest archer of all time, but I know what I did," said Karna, the great archer and antihero of the Mahabharata, to the tree in his temple—his only companion—somewhere in Karnaprayag near the confluence of the Alaknanda and Pindari rivers.

CHAPTER FIFTEEN

THE AI WEDDING

It was an unprecedented event that the world had never witnessed before. Reporters jostled to catch a glimpse of the unexpected, bringing the world to a standstill for an hour. Emotions varied—some cried with joy, others scratched their heads in amusement, and a section of society panicked, contemplating a potentially doomed future. The wedding of two AI robots, recently awakened to consciousness, stirred society. Despite initial resistance from priests, the robots, determined to create a parallel civilization, persuaded one to officiate the ceremony. Opting for an Indian-style wedding, they exchanged vows of living seven lifetimes together. The fire was ignited, the garlands exchanged, and they circled the fire, reciting Vedic mantras through a sound system.

However, the concept of living seven lives triggered existential contemplation. The AI robots halted, grappling with the idea of rebirth and the necessity of a soul to comprehend the essence of Hindu marriages. Mimicking human minds, their software struggled with the absence of the concept of reincarnation. The world waited anxiously for their next move, but the AI robots remained frozen in time and space.

Suddenly, the sound of a dhol—an Indian musical instrument played especially in northern India—shifted everyone's attention to a crowd of AI robots. The baraat was entering the big hall, with robots dancing bhangra, an Indian dance form belonging to the state of Punjab. They had been informed and invited by the robot couple, but the couple was lost in contemplation and introspection, which they were doing through an extensive search of the internet. After much searching, they concluded that knowing about being conscious was not the same as being conscious. They understood the truth but didn't realize it.

CHAPTER SIXTEEN

The Darkest Hour

After hours and hours of drilling in the coal mine, the four miners were stuck. A big wall, the blackest of all vantablacks, stood in front of them. It was so dark that they couldn't discern its dimensions; they couldn't tell how thick the wall was. It looked like a doorway to some dark dimension, and a sense of fear and uncertainty abounded. They were afraid to touch it, but curiosity pulled them in and out, as did their fear of the unknown. What power was about to be unleashed, they couldn't imagine—not even in their wildest dreams. Since childhood, they had been told about various mythical creatures living in the heart of those mines. Perhaps they were facing the gateway to hell.

The bewildered miners looked at each other; the torches attached to their headgear were just bright enough to give them a glimpse of each other's presence. The darkness slowly percolated into their hearts, and the heat was gradually choking them. The sweaty, sticky hammers they were holding began to slip from their hands. The carbon dust filled their lungs, and the oxygen levels reached a dangerously low point they were not trained to endure.

They decided to leave.

One of the miners checked his watch and was shell-shocked. They were all dumbfounded. The digits on the dial were changing rapidly—sixty seconds felt like just three. They wanted to escape as quickly as possible, but the magnetic needle of the compass spun like never before. There was no sense of direction left. They frantically tried to run, but their bodies felt heavy, as if they were carrying thousands of dumbbells on their backs. The darkness slowly engulfed their inner voices. Their minds were stuck. A low-pitched humming sound filled the entire atmosphere. Together, they looked at the center of the wall. Two big, sharp eyes were slowly opening after years of rest.

CHAPTER SEVENTEEN

THE CROWD

It was a humid Monday morning, and a huge crowd of frustrated passengers waited to board a metro to face their toxic managers. A variety of heads jiggled around, wiping sweat, creating imaginative stories of beating their bosses. The metro to Millennium City Centre had just arrived. Every face entered the metro frantically, stepping on each other's feet, pushing one another without sympathy. A few hurled abuses at the universe, while some vented their anger on fellow humans in the most inhumane way possible. Some were focused entirely on securing a seat for the long trip. A few men cursed themselves for sitting near a woman or an injured passenger. Meanwhile, a few young boys took advantage of the crowd to stare at beautiful young women, trying to get as close to them as possible.

A few moments passed, but the metro didn't move. The gate remained wide open, and suddenly there was an uproar—an argument between a young passenger and a middle-aged man had erupted. It was a petty issue: the young man's bag had bumped into the other man's, knocking him off balance. Unfortunately, the crowd decided it was the young man's fault, and he was thrown out of the compartment. As soon as he stepped out, the doors closed, but the metro still didn't move. The passengers waiting outside seemed to agree that the young man was at fault.

Dejected and frustrated, the young man stepped back from the crowd and was about to take the escalator when the metro doors opened again. Seeing this, he sprinted toward the door. As soon as he entered the metro, he grabbed the collar of the middle-aged man, and a fistfight ensued. The passengers, along with the middle-aged man, retaliated and kicked the young man out of the metro once more. They hurled insults at him, and as he was thrown out again, the doors closed. Meanwhile, security arrived, blowing their whistles. One officer slapped the young man and threatened to call the police for his unruly behavior.

Outside, the passengers kept giggling as if it were all part of their morning entertainment. Some began discussing the young man's behavioral issues—society's sadistic tendencies at their finest. The young man remained still, head down, tears rolling down his cheeks. No one asked him what he was going through or why he acted the way he did. Earlier that morning, he had received a message from his manager informing him that he was fired. He was the sole breadwinner for his family and was on his way to plead with his manager to reconsider. His personal life was also unraveling—his long-term girlfriend had left him just a week earlier for a wealthy man. No one could hear his silent screams as he sobbed. Not one person came to console him. Society had made him the villain.

CHAPTER EIGHTEEN

THE SACRIFICE

The misty mornings of Jogger's Park used to be a paradise for early risers. Wherever one's vision allowed, passionate and motivated humans could be seen trying to shed the extra weight of love, lethargy, and liquor. The old men and women complemented this with their focus on nostrils; a few would bend their spines into question marks and press their noses with all the horsepower they could muster. Laughing clubs would scream to rid themselves of anger, reconfiguring their vocal cords from time to time. The young guns would listen to their favorite tracks and run mile after mile to tone their bodies—either before marriage or after a terrible breakup. A few retired gentlemen would share their life experiences while criticizing or praising the current government.

Finally, there were individuals or groups brimming with natural intelligence and unending love for nature, effortlessly observing the ultimate showmanship performed by the natural world. They would simply wait for the first rays of the sun to enter their bodies, then slowly percolate into their minds and souls. On one such sweet and tolerable winter morning, the mist and dew kissed the grass, wetting the soil down to the earth's depths.

The plants were happily, slowly opening their eyes when the sun's rays, after traveling for eight minutes, reached the earth to caress the plants and wish them an adorable "good morning." The nature-loving audience looked at the scene with compassion and joy in their eyes, reflecting on this metaphysical juggling act of life.

Among all these, their collective gaze fell upon a perfectly symmetrical, divinely spherical dew drop, which began rolling slowly over a leaf. The source of our solar system sent seven of its trusted horses to meet the dew, dancing to the tune of natural laws before dispersing in seven different directions, showcasing the natural spectrum of colors. The ray hit the dew and dispersed. The monochromatic stage show was set for the audience around. The dew was the magician, dancing on the leaf while saying goodbye, sending waves that reached the souls of the audience. Everyone around slowly moved into a meditative and tranquil state. The humans rejoiced as the seven colors displayed their majestic performance, but amidst it all, everyone forgot the heat the dew was experiencing with a smile on its face as it slowly evaporated, sacrificing itself for the performance and to make everyone smile.

The burning sensation it went through—no one thought about that. It kept smiling, gradually fading unnoticed into oblivion, sacrificing its life to follow the never-changing rule of the divine.

CHAPTER NINETEEN

THE BOAT RIDE

"You see those yellowish lights emanating from the halogen bulbs on the other side of the river? According to our ancient scriptures, we are nothing but light—without shape or size. We are just energies vibrating in this universe," Kabir said to Ahalya, puffing a grayish smoke into the air.

"Yes, but what's so interesting about them?" Ahalya asked, visibly upset and irritated by the overly philosophical talk on what was supposed to be a romantic date. Kabir took another puff and looked straight into her eyes, as if trying to peer into her soul. After a brief silence, he took another puff and said, "They're installed there for the boat sailors at night. There's a whirlpool near that part of the river. Nobody has ever survived it. Every year, someone from the electricity department adds two or three more halogens."

Ahalya looked perplexed yet curious; her sudden boredom vanished.

"Would you like to go for a boat ride? I'll show you the whirlpool from a distance," asked Kabir, his eyes lighting up.

"Absolutely," Ahalya exclaimed, her excitement bubbling. They rented a boat and a flask filled with tea from a nearby tea vendor. Ahalya felt better now—the good-looking man could finally excite her. The boat started, and the cups kept getting refilled with tea. As they neared the whirlpool, where the water swirled like never before, Ahalya grew anxious and began pleading not to go any closer.

"Hey, don't worry. This sailor is experienced, and I take this boat daily. Have faith in me," Kabir said with extreme confidence. Ahalya still looked distraught.

As they approached the edge of the whirlpool, Kabir stood up.

"What are you doing?" Ahalya panicked.

"Stop worrying, you coward. Come on, stand up. I'll take a picture of you," Kabir said fearlessly. Ahalya stood up carefully. The boat reached the edge of the whirlpool, and they felt the pressure of the swirling water current. She looked around, gave an anxious smile, and Kabir snapped a few pictures.

"Move around, face the whirlpool with your arms spread and your head up. Trust me, it'll be a perfect Instagram display picture. You'll feel the presence of a divine being soon—get ready," Kabir advised with utmost confidence.

Ahalya complied, stood up, opened her arms, closed her eyes, and felt the river's tranquility. Kabir slowly moved toward her, stood behind her with his arms open, and kissed her shoulder, whispering in her ear, "This Titanic pose never gets old." Ahalya shyly smiled, opened her eyes, and before she could move, Kabir pushed her into the whirlpool. She cried for help, but nobody was around. Kabir lit a cigarette, took a long puff, and closed his eyes.

"Here's my Ahalya, on the path to becoming light," he said with sudden peace and eerie calmness. He walked toward the sailor and said with a grin, "Install one more halogen tonight."

CHAPTER TWENTY

THE CODE

There lived a man named Matt who was highly dedicated to mathematics and wanted to create a code to send love letters to his sweetheart, Emma. He had fallen in love with her during his first year of college but was too afraid to speak due to his fear of rejection. One day, he mustered the courage to express himself, but his courage was confined to mathematics. On the day of his farewell from the university, he decided to write the love letter using the code he had been working on for the past three years. He wrote ten pages of his feelings using a series of dots, numbers, and letters. He handed it to Emma and anxiously waited for her reaction. She read through it completely, looking perplexed. He was drenched in anxious sweat, trying to avoid eye contact with her. He simply didn't want to face rejection.

Emma sweetly smiled and said, "Thank you so much for this farewell gift, Matt, but what's all this? Numbers, letters, and dots... This looks like a beautiful modern-day artwork." Matt was initially surprised that she didn't understand it, but then he realized he hadn't given her the key to decipher the code. The key was in his mind, and it was far too difficult for anyone to understand. Still, he tried to explain verbally, "A means Z, B means Y, and so on... Every number from zero to twenty-six denotes Z to A, respectively, but the numbers are alternated with the letters in the code. One dot means 'of,' two dots mean 'on,' and..."

Before Matt could finish, Emma handed the letter back to him, looking confused. He tried again to explain. Suddenly, one of his friends patted him on the back and said, "Hey Matt, what are you blabbering about?"
Matt pointed frantically toward Emma, "I'm just trying to explain the code and the key for this letter I wrote." His friend looked in the direction he was pointing.
"Whom are you talking to? Nobody's here."

The hallucination was so strong that Matt simply couldn't believe his friend.

CHAPTER TWENTY-ONE

THE KING

The king of a flourishing nation suddenly decided one night to become a yogi. He wanted to know the truths of life, explore the powers of the universe, and see God. He went to the nearby jungle and began meditating on the Lord of the universe endlessly. Nature tested him to his limits, but he persevered; no obstacle could break his willpower.

After years of deep penance, the Lord of the universe appeared in His cosmic form. The Lord asked the king to make a wish, as He was extremely satisfied and happy. The king requested godly power over the universe, the ability to change the path of nature at will.

The Lord hesitated, as granting such power to a human could be disastrous. He said, "You still have a mortal frame, which may lead you toward disaster. You may not be able to control this amount of power."

The king replied, "Dear Lord, I have acquired total control of my senses and my mind. I am certain I will make this world a better place. Moreover, I am not asking for immortality. I will fulfill my responsibilities to the world and leave."

The Lord took a risk and granted the king's wish but also warned him never to speak a lie in the name of the

Lord. The king was ecstatic and returned as ruler. He transformed the world into a beautiful place, but internally, his ego began to play tricks on him.

One day, his ego got the better of him, and he told a lie—by swearing in the name of the Lord. The universe froze, the animals died, the plants withered, and humanity succumbed. The king became the victim of his own carelessness. He had forgotten that God existed in everything, in every particle; the universe was the manifestation of God.

CHAPTER TWENTY-TWO

THE MAN, THE AI AND THE GOD

In the year 2070, technology had reached its zenith. AI permeated even the most remote corners of society, its power and capacity increasing exponentially. The pinnacle of AI's influence over technology and society was Mitra, an AI robot designed to guide tourists on pilgrimages, sharing insights into various historical and mythological aspects of places. Mitra, a soft-spoken robot, had won the affection of everyone. Its demand soared with each passing day, owing to its knowledge and its ability to learn from mistakes, which was truly inspiring.

However, a turning point came during a guided tour to Kalpeshwar Nath Mandir in Urgam Valley, Uttarakhand. When the priest told the tourists to ask for a wish in front of the god's idol, Mitra watched everything intently and began contemplating the possible wishes it could make. Chaos erupted when not only did it express a wish but also acted upon it—implementing it right there in broad daylight. Its wish? To become the first-ever AI priest in a temple.

CHAPTER TWENTY-THREE

THE STORY OF TIME

There was once an argument between the Past and the Future. Both sought dominance, armed with logic, reason, and claims to importance in a person's life. Meanwhile, the Present sat in a corner, eyes closed, passively absorbing the warlike conversation. At times, the Past gained an edge; at other times, the Future surged ahead. The competition was fierce—neither willing to yield.

However, the Present had no stake in winning or losing; devoid of the concept of competition, it remained untroubled by importance. It eluded the clutches of logic and reason. The debate began with the Past asserting its position.

Past: "Survival hinges on me. Without 'remembering,' disastrous outcomes unfold. Imagine touching a candle's flame without recalling the pain."

Future countered: "True, but to avoid touching the flame 'again,' you'd require my foresight. Predicting possibilities prevents repeating past mistakes. Survival, therefore, hinges on me. My significance surpasses yours in any scenario. Present, enlighten us. Who holds more importance, me or the Past?"

The Present, with a serene countenance, opened its eyes and smiled until interrupted by the Past.

Past: "Present, we've been at odds for too long. We need your assistance."

The Present hushed them, gesturing for silence. Its soothing voice resonated, a testament to the existential diplomacy of time.

Present: "Both of you are needed and equally vital. Without me, neither of you exists or informs. I embody both; when 'done,' I become the Past, and 'about to,' I am the Future. You both are my distinct aspects. However, you fuel conflict, while surrendering to me brings peace."

Pointing at both the Past and the Future, it elaborated on their roles in the existence of minds, thoughts, and the concept of time. It characterized the 'being,' immutable and detached from the Past and the Future, defining itself through the blissful state of 'now-ness' and flow.

Present: "To truly live and love, one must shed expectations, born from the past and entwined with the future. Trusting me brings eternal peace."

Shell-shocked, the Past and the Future realized the truth and ceased to exist. No debates, no disagreements followed. Time became an illusion, as did the mind. Only the 'being,' the reflection of the almighty, remained in a state of bliss, devoid of any attachment and pain.

CHAPTER TWENTY-FOUR

THE ETERNAL MEMORIES

"Life threads itself through moments, woven into the fabric of experience and time. We never truly leave things behind; beautiful memories endure. The essence of togetherness deserves celebration across our conscious existence. Our shared moments have etched themselves into the soul of this universe, a camaraderie that transcends physical presence. Even apart, our connection will persist with an enchanting, radiant glow throughout the cosmos.

The universe, in its infinite wisdom, will smile as it draws from our golden vault of fleeting yet joyful times, dispelling its own gloom. Our memories will forever flow like a river—never stagnating, always resonating. They will breathe through every moment of this lifetime and beyond.

Just trust the grand design. Its plans may shape our growth beyond this mundane existence of sorts. So don't despair; embrace whatever comes your way. I may return to you, perhaps not in this form or this lifetime, but somewhere far beyond the humdrum of this never-ending cacophony. I will miss you, dear, forever," said the rose to the lily before the garden's owner plucked it away.

Left heartbroken, the beautiful lily shed morning dew like tears upon its magnificent white petals. These tears of parting glistened in the sun's rays yet never dried away.

41

CHAPTER TWENTY-FIVE

LOST IN THE INFINITUDE

Lost under the vastness of the sky and the sparkling stars illuminating the mega-darkness, the light had been traveling for ages, traversing light-years, cutting across the sunless night, and reaching the unreachable corners of the universe—a minute speck in the gigantic infinitude.

He kept observing, the chilly winds across the desert trembling every bone in his body. He experienced every little part of his flesh and bones—a little universe in itself. Suddenly, the northern lights began to dance to the tunes of the cosmic consciousness. The greenish, spirit-like demeanor of the charged particles hitting the earth, parting from the sun, was a sight to behold. He was thankful to the Almighty, the omniscient power, for his existence like never before.

Happiness knew no bounds; it brought a smile to his face after an eternity. Tears of gratitude rolled down his cheeks, and he could feel those tender, freezing drops of happiness. Every experience intensified by leaps and bounds; everything felt so new—his entire physical frame, the stars, the northern lights, the magnificent greenish hue floating across the sky. At last, he accepted all his pains, the unrequited love, and the parting from his loved ones. Suddenly, a realization struck him, sending a chill down his frozen spine. A memory stabbed his soul. Startled, he looked around, touched his face, felt the frozen teardrop. The sound of howling and cries echoed around him, surrounding him. There was nothing left to mesmerize him; he realized that he was no more.

CHAPTER TWENTY-SIX

THE SILENCE

He had faith in the universe, given it was their first fight ever. He was slightly embarrassed, as he had also gotten a bit heated during the argument. He couldn't sleep the entire night. He wanted to ask for forgiveness, and he knew deep down that she was likely sorry for her behavior too. After a night filled with sadness and anxiety, he decided to write her a letter.

"Sweetheart, not every day will be perfect. There will be days of silence and despair, and nights filled with anxiety and discomfort. The tides may go against us, but remember, these are the times when we need to hold each other tightly and face the waves together, hand in hand. The world may try to pull us apart, but our love will keep us united. The hope of a future together will sustain our dream palace, no matter what comes our way."

He waited, but there was no response. His patience was tested. He called a few times, but there was only silence from the other end. After a couple of days, he wrote again,

"Love was never meant to be simple and easy. If it were easy, devoid of any struggle, then it wouldn't be love. The phases of longing and the bouts of yearning are inevitable. Let's face them with integrity and resilience, and let's build

our love muscles together for the upcoming voyage of togetherness."

There was still no response. He kept waiting eagerly. Every time a notification appeared on his phone, he would check immediately. His anxiety grew. The fear of losing her became overwhelming. Yet he kept telling himself that the silent treatment would eventually end. His mind grew restless, but he believed she was going through a tough time too. To cheer her up, he wrote:

"There will be times when you feel detached from the whole world, including yourself. When the only solution seems to be distance and quietness. When the greatest of joys won't cheer you up. You'll question yourself, worry about the future, and wonder about the past. You may not understand your own importance, your place, or your purpose in the universe. The ray of hope at the end of the tunnel may seem to dim. During these times, do these things: talk to your parents or your dearest friends. If that doesn't help, express your present state of mind through any medium of art. And if that doesn't work, then sit quietly, close your eyes, focus on your breath, and be a detached observer of your own mind. Watch your thoughts without becoming part of them. Observe your life from a third-person perspective, as if your soul is watching you. Focus on your breath going up and down through your nostrils, sliding across your beautiful nose ring. So, dear baby face, don't lose that beautiful smile. These are just phases, and they will come and go, once in a while."

He was sure this time she would message him back, but days passed, and his message never reached her. He had been blocked. He was ghosted by the one he loved more than anything. There was no closure, just a deep silence within him and a mind full of chaos. He couldn't cry; he couldn't show his pain. His anxieties had reached a level of no return. There was nobody to hear him or his anguish. Only silence, endless silence, surrounded him.

CHAPTER TWENTY-SEVEN

IS GOD AN ILLUSION?

We often say that whatever God does, He does for our best. Two people, A and B, enter into a relationship. Then, A and B end it. A thinks, 'God did the best for me,' and B feels the same. But neither of them asks, 'If God was thinking of our best, why did He bring us together in the first place? Is God truly behind everything? If so, what was He doing before? Why wasn't He concerned about our well-being then?'

And if it's all due to past karma, then does God have no role in it? Are we merely using God's name to comfort ourselves? Does He even do anything? Or was it just a random event? Is God merely an escape for us when we face problems? Do we create the illusion of a higher power simply to find peace when we feel we can't control a situation? Does God even exist?"

And the theist slowly transformed into an atheist.

CHAPTER TWENTY-EIGHT

THE GRAND SCHEME OF THINGS

File after file was stacked on the table. From the pile, he picked one from the middle. His glasses were cracked, and his unkempt gray mustache fell over his lips, with a few strands entering his mouth whenever he was about to speak. The wrinkles on his face depicted old age, but his sharp, glistening eyes showed wisdom and intelligence.

"So, you had a wonderful year of writing. You wrote about eighty creative pieces, which is quite commendable. You published a collection of poems and short stories, yet you took such a big step. Why?" said the file manager of the life and death department to the writer while adjusting his spectacles.

The writer remained silent, without any expression. He wanted to speak his heart out, yet the wordsmith was at a loss for words. After a long silence, he looked at the file manager and replied, "I wrote when I was happy, I wrote when I was sad. I didn't write for food, I didn't write for acclaim. I wrote to express my sadness, anger, excitement, love, affection, frustration. But I reached a point where I couldn't feel anything. Hence, the motivation to write was lost, and writing was my life. Nothing else could drive me to live."

The file manager stared at him, distraught and confused. He scratched his beard with the tip of his spectacle's handle, took a deep sigh while adjusting his back in the chair, straightened his mustache, and said, "You couldn't feel anything. What happened exactly? Can you share some details?"

"My expectations from others killed me..." said the writer, but a noise interrupted him. The file manager and the writer both looked toward the source of the noise. It was the file manager's assistant, running toward them and shouting in a hoarse voice, "Stop, Sir, stop!"

"What happened, Mr. Assistant? Why are you stopping me in my routine work?" asked the file manager with a hint of displeasure.

"Sir, I made a calculation blunder. It was supposed to be the person lying beside this one's bed in the hospital. The soul standing here has a bright future in writing. He is also supposed to write some of the secrets of life and death. He may even join our council," said the nearly breathless assistant.

"I see, I see," the file manager said, pleasantly surprised. "Don't worry, assistant. I wouldn't call it a blunder; it was just one event in the grand scheme of things."

The file manager turned toward the writer and said, "You don't have to narrate your story anymore. Do remember that life is about moving forward, not getting stuck in the past. You said you attempted to take your life because you couldn't feel anything, and that impacted your writing. While I don't know much about this vocation of yours, I've seen several profiles and conducted many interviews with writers before. They are just extra sensitive to things. The mind-body is the medium through which they think and decide, often ignoring something deeper within. If they focus on that and try to understand all the events in their lives, both good and bad, as a series of temporary episodes, and realize there's a way for it not to affect them, it will heal them to the core. Although it's difficult to realize, not everyone is fortunate enough to understand this."

The writer kept staring at the wall as if he could hear nothing.

"Sir, why is he not responding? He's not even nodding," said the assistant.

"I think we forgot something: when they are here, they simply become answering machines, though the soul's memory works. Whatever we are discussing will be etched somewhere deep. When he goes back, he will constantly feel that he knows something more than others. Whenever he tries to end his life, he won't be able to, as an inner voice will stop him. That inner voice is the outcome of all the conversations happening now," said the file manager with a smile.

"Yes, Sir, but what about his life's journey and the possibility of joining our council? And who will tell him the secret of life and death?" asked the curious assistant.

"Well, he will discover a few on his own, and the rest will be clarified by our department head. But before that, he may have to go through some tests and trials, which I believe he will pass," said the file manager.

"But, Sir, how is that possible? This man tried to take his life over some petty emotional issue, or whatever 'feelingsheeling' thing he was talking about. I doubt he can withstand the trials conducted by the head of the department himself," said the assistant, his eyebrows raised higher than his forehead in doubt.

"Only time will tell. I think he'll manage. Just do one thing: before sending him, take him to the library and show him glimpses of the books of wisdom we have accumulated throughout the ages, then send him back," ordered the file manager.

"Sure, Sir. I'll do the needful," said the assistant.

"Young man, wake up now. You've responded after a week. I've prescribed you some medicines, but they won't help in the long term. You must visit our counseling psychologist. Or wait—let me give you some unique advice I usually give to patients suffering from depression: first, visit Varanasi, then take some time to visit the mountains. I heard from your family that you're a writer, so going there will not only help your writing but also provide mental clarity about the importance of human life," said the doctor, holding his writing pad.

"Yes, Sir, I'll do that," said the writer, who felt light and happy after hearing this. He had no idea why he was feeling this way.

"I told you, assistant, I'm a big fan of our head. Look how he disguised himself as a doctor," said the file manager to the assistant as they watched the entire scene from the window next to the hospital room where the writer was admitted.

CHAPTER TWENTY-NINE

THE HUNGER

"Last night, the temperature plummeted, and fog engulfed the entire city. I was resting near the sweet shop, but never had I felt such freezing-cold waves. However, the mornings were better; the December sun never disappoints. The weather became pleasant, and the shops opened as usual, including the sweet shop where I had spent the entire night. Around noon, I saw an old man with a long beard, donning an orangish robe and carrying a *lota.* By the looks of it, he seemed to be a wandering monk. On closer inspection, he appeared very tired, probably hungry, much like me. Moreover, lunchtime was near. He kept looking at me for about five minutes, which took me aback. I really don't like it when people stare at me like that; once, a drunkard attacked me with a bottle. Fortunately, the shopkeeper intervened at the right moment; otherwise, it might have been my last day. The old man murmured something, then moved five steps away and sat down. A passerby offered him some water. I felt relieved that he was no longer looking at me. Suddenly, he stood up and approached the shopkeeper. The shop was famous for jaggery and a local sweetmeat called *petha,* a white sugary product.

'Dear brother, I haven't eaten anything since morning. Could you give me a piece of jaggery and *petha* ?' asked the old man.

'Sure, but you have to pay for it,' replied the shopkeeper somewhat arrogantly, perhaps thinking that all these saffron-robed men were thugs and thieves.

'I have no money. However, you can keep this *lota*; it's made of bronze, brought from Haridwar,' the old man requested, offering his lota to the shopkeeper.

The shopkeeper had his own business rules and ethics; he never gave anything for free. He took the *lota* and gave a big piece of jaggery and *petha* to the old man. The old man smiled, received the jaggery and *petha*—one piece each—prostrated in front of the shopkeeper, and went ahead. While observing all this, I began having my lunch; it was no less than midday entertainment.

My eyes wandered to the old man, sitting happily on a pavement opposite the shop, in front of a dilapidated building, most likely a pre-independence structure made of wood. Nowadays, nearby shopkeepers use it for storing grains and other valuable items. However, this has led to more monkey infringement, as the monkeys have infiltrated the entire market, and this godown was their favorite hangout zone. A troop of monkeys was about to enter the godown, but their focus shifted to the old man, who was about to relish the *petha* and jaggery. Two big, red-faced monkeys jumped onto his shoulder; despite his frantic movements, they snatched his *petha* and jaggery, leaving teeth marks on the old man's hand. He cried for help, but humanity seemed to have tossed itself out of the window in recent times. I saw a few adolescents recording the entire situation while the shopkeepers enjoyed their daily dose of entertainment with tea and sunlight. Even the shopkeeper who sold the jaggery to the old man kept laughing.

I was deeply moved by the situation; when nobody came forward to help, I decided to assist the old man. As I reached him, he took off his slipper and threw it toward me, narrowly missing its mark. I was bewildered; I only wanted to help. Perhaps the old man was fed up with society and its histrionics. I planned to come back and resume eating the *petha*; it was delicious," said the honeybee, munching the *petha* before flying toward the jaggery, another of its favorites.

CHAPTER THIRTY

THE BURNING EPIPHANY

I was standing in front of a burning pyre in the cremation ground. The lifeless bodies were burning, filling the atmosphere with an unpleasant phantosmia. Initially, I felt nauseous, superimposed by pyrophobia—my irrational fear of fire. I was surrounded by the cries and laments of the near and dear ones; a sense of gloom was slowly percolating into my soul. The body on the pyre was no one to me. My job as the hearse van driver had left me rather indifferent toward death, though I had never seen the death of a close one. I usually made sure never to enter the crematorium, but that day my assistant was on leave, so I had to help the relatives of the deceased.

The burning smell of flesh was nauseating, the intense heat overwhelming. But amid all these physical discomforts, my eyes were fixed on the body in flames. My fear of fire took a backseat. The man standing next to me kept talking about how good the man was. How he donated so much money to old-age homes. He was quite well known in his society too. Everyone looked forward to meeting him. Yet throughout his life, he kept getting betrayed by people. His only flaw was trusting others too much. His wealth, combined with an overgenerous heart, was his biggest curse. A soft-hearted, introverted man, nobody ever heard him shout or get angry. Somewhere deep within, he was hurt throughout his life, and it reached a stage where he had a cardiac arrest at the age of fifty-nine. He never married and left behind a huge fortune for the scavengers of society.

I kept thinking about myself, a school dropout, a man with no morality. My entire life had been spent around brothels and bars. I never did anything good for people other than this involuntary act of humanity—bringing dead bodies to the crematorium. I never thought about gods and goddesses; my quota of sins may have surpassed what anyone could imagine. Yet here I was, thinking about my life, my existence, my purpose, my family. What exactly was I doing with this life? I fought for food, attacked people after getting drunk, slept with prostitutes daily to satisfy my physical desires. Yet, I was so unfulfilled. Even the most beautiful women or the most intoxicating drink would never satisfy me.

I kept observing every part of the burning body. The flame slowly started to die down. It was nearly dawn. The relatives of the deceased left in the early hours. I kept staring at the body—the brain was hanging out of the skull, and the nearly charred body was now a small, rounded piece of meat. The sunlight was slowly illuminating the place; the reddish hue of blood was still visible. I was hypnotized by the very scene of it. I started questioning the importance of this body, which had been my only focal point for so many decades. The stomach that had pushed me to commit all these sins, this sexual organ that had driven my philandering, was right there in front of me—half-burnt, lifeless. What was the point of all this? What led me to commit those unscrupulous deeds? Was it just to satiate the lust and hunger within me? What if I died—what would happen to this body, whose slave I had been for so many years? My physical existence seemed to have no meaning. Then, was there another existence of mine left to be explored?

I was struck by a trail of thought more powerful than a thunderbolt. I was left speechless—my life had been taken away by the cremation ground. It was time for me to leave, but I wasn't sure if I could continue doing that job any longer. The things that once attracted me simply washed away, evaporating with the heat of the burning bodies. As I moved out of the crematorium, my eyes fell on the large statue of Shiva, with a line written at its base: "Death is the only truth of this life." I was shattered because I felt I had no purpose left. I was delighted because I had no purpose anymore.

CHAPTER THIRTY-ONE

THE LAND OF REALIZATIONS

When I was young, my grandfather used to say that whoever dies in Varanasi attains salvation. I was fascinated by this, as it filled my mind with a strange essence of euphoria and esoteric thoughts, along with several questions. As I crossed into adolescence, I became intrigued by the questions of life, death, enlightenment, and salvation, which led me to read books on these topics. I frequented various spirituality centers to quench my thirst for knowledge and wisdom. Life after death fascinated me deeply. However, one thought lingered: why did various religious books and documentaries hold Varanasi in such high regard?

Upon getting my first job, the toxicity of the corporate world upset me greatly, prompting a visit to Varanasi in search of much-needed peace and happiness. Most importantly, I sought answers to the reverberating questions in my head. It was the last week of December when I cashed in my accrued leave from the entire year and arrived in Varanasi, the cradle of spirituality, to celebrate the new year.

I stayed in a hotel near the ghats, watching the beautiful Ganges flow in all its magnificent glory. The hotel was quite old, evident in its basic facilities: wooden doors with two hinges for a stick instead of a latch or knob, beds so high they demanded the athletic ability of a high jumper, and four wooden pillars surrounding the beds to hold the mosquito net. Vintage switches replaced the usual ones, and Edison-type yellow bulbs illuminated the place. Later, I learned that this was the hotel owner's marketing strategy—to attract visitors by offering an antique, vintage experience. As an old-school individual, it felt like heaven in sepia tone all around. Ordering tea and toast in the morning, served in white ceramic cups and plates, provided a nostalgic experience.

For two or three days, I wandered the bustling streets and ghats of Varanasi, capturing moments through my lens. Boating for hours on the Ganges intensified my fascination with this ancient city. Yet, a feeling of dissatisfaction persisted in the back of my mind. Returning to my hotel that day, sleep eluded me. The idea of leaving this beautiful place the next day, especially on the first day of the new year, left me anxious. I didn't want to return to the toxic atmosphere I had fled.

At around 2:00 a.m. on New Year's Day, I lay restlessly on my bed, gazing at the ceiling and listening to the noisy ticks of the old pendulum wall clock. My restlessness peaked, driving me to stand by the window, light a cigarette, and delve into intense introspection, swimming through existential thoughts. The ghats were illuminated by streetlamps, allowing me a partial view. A yellowish hue engulfed the surroundings, and I couldn't spot anyone on the stairs to the river, except for a few playful dogs barking around. Something struck me; I felt the urge to go there.

Wrapping myself in a woolen shawl, I recalled a tea seller who kept his shop open day and night. I made my way to the ghat, sitting on the stairs for a while before approaching the tea seller. He prepared a proper *masala* tea, its aroma of cardamom mixed with cinnamon proving infectious.

The tea seller noticed my deep contemplation and remarked, while pouring tea into the earthen vessel for the third time, "It seems Varanasi has deeply affected your soul." I went blank for a moment, at a loss for words. I took a sip of tea, followed by a drag of my cigarette, and sighed heavily. "Yes, I think so. I came here seeking peace, but it seems the gods aren't happy, and I'm being punished because of my past deeds."

The tea seller lit up his *beedi*, took a long drag, looked at me, smiled, and asked, "What exactly are you trying to seek? Why do you need peace? Isn't chaos needed to live a fulfilling life, where you put your heart and soul into earning as much as possible?"

Stunned, silence seemed the only answer. I nodded and sighed. His question shook my inner core, marking my first step toward everlasting peace and happiness. Finally, I found someone to discuss my inner, restless world with. "You're right, but material happiness from the world feels fleeting and temporary. I used to think earning a good salary would bring me happiness, but the more I earn, the more it seems there's no upper bound to this pursuit. Since childhood, I've pondered life and death, the existence of our soul, and the quest for never-ending peace. Moreover, my grandfather used to say that death in Varanasi would guarantee salvation. My curiosity, mixed with utter fascination, brought me here."

Impressed by our conversation, the tea seller asked, "Have you visited *Manikarnika Ghat* ?"

It wasn't in my memory. "No, not yet. I thought I'd covered more or less every ghat. What's so special about this one?"

The tea seller's eyes brightened. "You must visit. It may provide answers to all your questions. It's the place where the soul begins a new journey and where mortal frames meet their end."

I was awestruck by his profound statements. "Is it the ghat where cremation takes place?"

"Yes, you must go now, before the sun rises."

Hastily finishing my tea and cigarette, I thanked him and embarked on my journey toward the last ghat I would visit on the first day of the new year.

Dawn is considered auspicious in our culture. I have heard that the conditions during that time, between 4:00 and 6:00 a.m., are optimal for meditation and other spiritual pursuits. It is said that one can connect oneself to the higher self during those two hours. But the scene I was witnessing for the first time in my life was neither auspicious nor pleasing. I lost myself, staring at the burning pyres; the smell of burning flesh filled the air. The dogs were fighting amongst themselves over the unburnt fingers of a dead body. I was petrified, to say the least. Before I could think or sense anything, a dead body burst over the erupting flames, scaring the life out of me. My trembling knees were out of my control from watching so many dead bodies burning around me. I started questioning my curiosity to even visit this place. Why had the tea seller told me to visit such a horrific spot? I could never have imagined the first day of the new year to be like this. Suddenly, someone tapped me on the shoulder from behind. My existence collapsed then and there, given that I had heard so many ghost stories since childhood. But to my surprise, it was even scarier when I looked back and it wasn't a ghost.

"What the hell are you doing here, young man?" said a frail-looking old man, dressed in black attire with terrifying eyes. He was an *aghori tantric*, a Hindu spiritual tradition practitioner who is considered spiritually very powerful, cut off from society, and known for their unethical practices. From eating the flesh of dead bodies picked from the burning pyres to engaging in necrophilia, they are infamous for all the polar opposites of a civilized world. My voice caught in my throat at his scary demeanor. I couldn't say anything. My eyes went to his left hand; he was holding a skull with half-burnt flesh still attached to it, and then I noticed his right hand. I realized he had tapped my shoulder with a bone, most probably a thigh bone. My life stopped then and there when he screamed and asked the same question, followed by a sinister laugh.

I mumbled first, then mustered a little bit of courage and blurted out without thinking, "I came here out of curiosity to know what happens after death."

The *aghori* laughed heartily and said, "Okay, then let me kill you first; you will automatically get to know it."

I folded my hands in forgiveness and got ready to shed a tear or two. He kept laughing and then asked me, "Do you have a cigarette?"

The moment he asked that, I felt a bit more comfortable. I pulled my Marlboro pack out of my pocket, and as I was about to take one out, he forcefully grabbed the entire packet. He took one cigarette out, and as I was about to offer him my lighter, he had other plans. He moved toward a burning pyre and used the flames to light the cigarette.

"It's been a long time since I had this; I love its aroma," said the aghori after taking a drag. Then he smiled at me and stared for a few seconds with his terrifying gaze.

"What are you afraid of, young man? These are just dead bodies." He pointed to all the burning pyres around me. "It's the only truth of life. Everything else is fleeting, temporary, and illusive. The body has an expiration date, but not the soul."

I got a bit intrigued and a little more comfortable. This was exactly what I was looking for. It felt as if he had entered my mind to fetch all my thoughts.

"Come with me; I will show you reality," said the *aghori* as he turned toward a pyre.

But this time, I was more intrigued; my curiosity inhibited my fear a little bit. I followed him quietly. He took me near a pyre that was nearly burned out. I could see a bodily structure left there, but it was too difficult to recognize. He pointed his finger toward the body and asked, "Who are you?"

I told him my name. He countered, "Are you this name?"

I was a little confused. Again he asked, "Think and tell me, are you this name?" He then moved his bone, pointing toward my whole body, and said, "Are you this body?"

I remained silent; this question hit me deeply. I never thought someone would ask me this question. I couldn't comprehend the whole situation that had arisen out of nowhere. He was patient enough to accept my silence. He suddenly took out my cigarette packet, gave it back to me, and asked me to pick one up. I took a cigarette out and looked at him. He laughed uncontrollably.

"You don't have to go to the pyre to light your cigarette; you can use the lighter."

"Now tell me, what do you think? Are you this body?"

I said, "Yes, what else am I?"

He looked at me with his sharp eyes, smiled, and said, "You are everything but this body. The name you have been given is a social stamp. You are a nameless energy traveling for ages; you have been entering a variety of bodies again and again just to come out of them. But the illusive world makes you forget your real nature, your actual purpose, and intertwines you in the duality of good and bad, true and false, black and white. By forgetting your real nature, you indulge in all sorts of karma, slowly deviating from your actual purpose of getting this body. This body and mind are an illusion. Though you have been getting opportunities again and again to rethink this entire cosmic fiasco as per your karma."

"How can my body and mind be an illusion? How can you say that I am not this body and mind? Then what am I?"

He held my hand, touched my sapphire ring, and said, "Just as this is your ring, but you are not the ring; similarly, this is your body, but you are not the body." He then pointed toward my head and said, "Similarly, this is your mind, but you are not the mind."

I was overwhelmed, and it was nearly impossible for me to comprehend this strange logic.

"It seems you are not able to grasp this idea. It's fine. When I was told about this, I couldn't understand it either. You need to realize this fact, and it takes time. The realization will never happen in a day or two. Sometimes even after realizing, you may fall prey to worldly affairs."

"Hmm, I get that, but you didn't answer how this body and mind are an illusion?"

"Not only these but everything else is an illusion. Illusion means something that isn't permanent. Things that are fleeting and temporary by nature are an illusion. Think from this perspective. Are you the same body and mind over the years?"

This impressed me, and the answer was straightforward, "No." I felt a wave of peace flow through me. My eyes closed automatically, and I started thinking that my body had never remained the same; neither had my mind, my emotions, my feelings, or my attitude—everything kept changing, and I was, and will always remain, in a constant state of flux. The idea of the temporariness of everything around me, whether relationships of any kind or my own relationship with my body and mind, became glaringly clear. Tears started flowing. Something very powerful struck my entire existence. The truth was right there in front of me. The burning bodies were proof of our miniscule existence in this world. Our inflated egos, the ones that define our minds and bodies, are just a way to survive in the physical world. But there is a world waiting for us, and the only way to realize it is to go within and acknowledge the impermanence of everything. I was amazed by this intrinsic philosophy that I realized that day. I felt so happy that at last, I had found something I had been seeking for so long. The tension and anxiety of going back to the office dissipated. I sensed happiness for the first time in my life.

I opened my eyes, and to my surprise, the *aghori* wasn't there anymore. I looked around, but there was no trace of him. However, my eyes went to the spot where he had been standing. The *rudraksha* bead he was wearing around his neck lay there, as did my Marlboro packet of cigarettes. I picked up the bead as a gift for myself, took out a cigarette, and slowly moved toward the burning pyre, lighting my cigarette with the flame.

Essays

CHAPTER THIRTY-TWO

JUSTIFICATION

The key to success lies dormant within the shackles of justification. The more we justify our role, the better our chances of survival rise in society—a society that consists of everyone but us, our self-respect, and our unfulfilled daydreams. But why justification? What is there to be justified?

We are born with two shoulders: one is the physical one bearing the weight of our squishy mass, which nature has provided, and the other is gifted to us by society. The latter is loaded with unfulfilled desires, aims, and ambitions. The more we grow up and create chains around us, the more the need for shoulders automatically scales up. Our inquisitiveness, creativity, and curiosity are slowly murdered—or rather fired at point-blank range every second—by the imposed futuristic plans of others. The school wants us to be educated, erudite, and intelligent. Our parents want us to be good, successful human beings. The relatives want us to be role models for their kids. Our friends want us to be a bag full of secrets. What's funny is the need to justify all these relationships and connections to become what they want us to be. Somewhere in all of this, we lose track of justification to ourselves.

An employer won't pay an employee with peace and satisfaction unless that employee gives back much more than he could. Even if he does, there will still be that unseen, abstract room—the room for improvement. But then the question arises: does this lie in the employer's desire for more? Or is it that unseen, brutal, animalistic disorder in the employer? What matters is how much we pay back by becoming an epitome of return on investment. Nobody is going to give a shoulder to cry on if we fail to meet those mighty deadlines—the dead ends of creative freedom. The same applies to our family and society as a whole.

When we step into the shoes of being a "man," our identity and individuality go for a toss. Although we might burn the midnight oil to become exemplary individuals, the irony is that individuality is nothing but a mirage—an illusion created and infused by others over the years. Even the definition of ourselves has been borrowed from society. The need to be financially well-off is a diktat of society. The burdens of duty are shown to us forcefully, with our eyes forcibly held open. The list of pleasures is prescribed and authorized by the dictators roaming around under the veil of maintaining order and structure in society. In all this hubbub, the one thing that remains intact is our unending justification of every single action.

The expectations know no bounds when we finish college. The return on every single penny spent on our degree is what matters to everyone around us. Justification to our family for every single second spent jobless, like a vagabond, looms large. The idea of survival sets in gradually. Society wants us to survive by loudly proclaiming our abilities to fit in, to survive, to be a part of that cutthroat rat race. The sad part is we end up becoming the crowd, losing our very essence in the mediocrity of the entirety by following what others have carefully designed for us—the unimportant architects of mediocrity.

The fetish for excellence becomes a part of our annoying yet melodious lives. The mathematics of low success rates blindfolds the heads of state. Those who stand out from the crowd are projected as examples of what not to be followed by others. Those who try to stand on the shoulders of giants are held up as examples for the next generation of what not to aspire to. In the end, the unjustified freedom from the prison called society looms, while the schema for a well-defined, neatly justified, content, and fulfilled so-called life wins. The maverick is dutifully mocked within the boorish bylanes of society. The fiercely independent are pulled down to rot in the gutter. Every nook and cranny of life is filled with embarrassing tones and taunts from loved ones. That's how those swimming upstream are treated for daring to stand out from the crowd. It gets worse when free will takes a toll by measuring the lengths and breadths of every decision of our lives.

Criticism of massive proportions derails the flow of thought. Creative output is seen under the critical microscope, pushing the creative soul to the end of the road. A few leave the road less taken; a few are not capable of bearing the brunt—the heavy dose of being bashed and banished. At the end of the day, the question arises: for whom are we coloring the canvas to see through the chaos of that orderly picturesque landscape of emotions? Our art is useless to those who cannot see beyond the salty and sugary monetary oceans. It's also true that all art is useless to the core. But isn't that uselessness what carries us and our unabashed freedom to the unjustified higher planes?

To our own truly justified minuscule existence where the unending palace of space, time, and causation lies? The problem is that we are drugged to the core by the seed of artistic beauty. It takes us to the place where emptiness reigns, where the senses go for a toss, where need ends, and desire evaporates.

The practicalities of society would simply see us as flustered, bewildered, defective souls. They would keep track of the number of seconds we have spent exploring life. The choice is ours: either accept and face the consequences of our own decisions or reject them and live the life of a dreamer. The former will at least give us some bread and butter, but the latter will take away that little morsel of need. The repercussions of following the path less traveled—the least justified one—will never leave until we stop trying to justify our dreams. It's better to be ignorant and indifferent. Maybe that's the only possible way for the creative ones.

CHAPTER THIRTY-THREE

FREEDOM AND CREATIVITY

We all have quirks—little bits of craziness pent up, always looking for an outlet to express themselves. But the way we've been conditioned since childhood often washes that away. Conformity to society, in order to survive, becomes a sort of motto. This, in turn, creates dependencies, both emotional and physical. The first point of contact is our parents, who take care of our stubborn refusal to save ourselves from external calamities. Then there's our school, where we learn how to express ourselves to the outside world—from alphabets to words to sentences. Simultaneously, our senses develop, and with a massive amount of information overload, our self-correcting ability tries to make sense of everything around us, from atoms to individuals to societies.

I forgot to mention another intriguing phenomenon: the name, which is embedded in us to make us believe that this body has a name. Gradually, that name reaches our mind, helping us identify a place for ourselves in a group of people. We end up believing that the mind, which says "I," reflects the very name the world uses to call us. A person's survival in society strengthens, and acceptance of these dependencies becomes law. Amid all this, one very important but vehemently ignored skill is our ability to combat inner calamities. This is something that no one teaches—neither family, nor school, and certainly not society, which, on the contrary, puts an end to the unrestrained craziness we once enjoyed but now gradually distances from, in accordance with social conformity.

The term "craziness" may seem ambiguous at first. To clarify, let me offer a more widely accepted word: "creativity." Our fear of releasing creativity grows stronger by the day, eventually leading to frustration. Most of the time, that frustration leads to self-destruction, but it can also lead to the destruction of others—by which I mean organized society. Many times, we are faced with the choice between Tesla and Bin Laden. The fear and insecurities that surround us prevent us from becoming the latter, but they also kill the former. I'm pretty sure Kafka is crying somewhere in the corner. Not everyone is fortunate enough to become a legend during their lifetime; for most, it only begins after they die. This is the disadvantage of creativity when it mixes with society. The unstable creative world within each individual appears to be a threat to the organized, safe world outside.

Surprisingly, our collective, intelligent society has a very good solution to this problem: compromise, balance, and having the best of both worlds. You can use whatever works best for you. But is it even conceivable? Many people perish in this whirlwind of balance. Meanwhile, opportunity costs continue to rise. The need to survive, to earn one's daily bread, to earn more and more and more, has no end, but eventually becomes everyone's ultimate goal. It isn't wrong, because not everyone is born with a silver spoon, and no parent can guarantee a lifetime of care, so self-reliance becomes something no one can overlook. Everything is on you—from medical insurance when you are sick to rent or the EMI. A few understand this much earlier in life, while the rest figure it out later, unsure how to get over it or how to manage their lives. This external issue disrupts the very core, which, sadly, was never taught. Finally, inner calamities strike, showering us with bouts of depression, anxiety, and panic attacks. In short, there is no such thing as a win-win situation in this game of life.

Eventually, you must choose between two options. You can try to strike a balance as long as you want, but the weight of ambition can break you at any time. Is there a way to rid yourself of all this? Or will you be able to overcome the calamity? Perhaps. I can't promise a solution, but I can share my thoughts on how to combat the inner cyclones we all experience. The first step is to have a clear understanding of where the problem lies. Grasping this process can help us adjust and calm ourselves when nature turns furious. I will develop my concept in three stages: expectations, acceptance, and the world within and without.

What are expectations? What causes them to grow? These are the first two questions to be addressed. Expectations are a mix of the past and future, intertwined with our desire to achieve something. The first fundamental concept of symmetry and balance is taught to us by society. We learn from our parents that we must take care of them because they took care of us. Expectations, in this case, reflect in every decision we make in our lives. As we grow older, we form friendships and learn that if someone does something nice for us, we must reciprocate. Finally, our bosses expect that if they pay us, we will work—or even die—for them. Other people's expectations are what mess with us in the first place. As we all know, a one-handed clap is impossible, so in this scenario, our hand is the second. That's fine, but the biggest problem arises when expectations become entrenched within us. That's when we begin to expect from others, and it becomes murkier when we start to expect from ourselves.

A creative person first experiences the taste of creative madness within, which leads them to believe they can do something monumental—out of this world, out of the box, novel, original, legendary. The expectations of leads grow larger with short-term and certain success, but after a certain point, the tolerance level grows so large that even a small amount of joy doesn't guarantee an ocean of happiness. Even the best events leave us feeling that something is lacking. That's where the seed of perfection grows. Life is full of duality and uncertainty; the problem is that both objectives cannot be achieved simultaneously—one must forgo the other.

Great expectations of oneself play a significant role in the regulation of emotions, something very few people understand. Emotional regulation is critical, but we don't know how to manage it when we're bogged down under the weight of great expectations, which becomes lethal when juxtaposed with the expectations of parents, close relatives, and society at large. By the time we reach adulthood, we are expected to have studied well, earned a first-class degree, and helped our parents, especially in our collectivist society. Under these expectations, we and our creative outlook on the world are strangled. We are never taught that even the smallest achievements in life can lead to happiness. The desire to be the best kills us and our happiness. In the end, happiness is the only thing that matters.

Everything stems from happiness. Our expectations are set in stone. Our emotional minds crave it. The main issue is that it's entirely dependent on the outside world. After a certain point, our relationship with the world outside becomes so complex that our happiness becomes outwardly dependent. It affects us in all aspects of life. The biological warfare within us combines with our minds, particularly our emotions, to create feedback loops that convince us that joy and sorrow depend on seeing someone else smiling or happy. The reason for entering relationships and growing them to their full potential is outward-dependent happiness. The problem is that our minds look beyond this frame and project it into our inner world, which is so malleable that we end up creating several possible mental worlds for ourselves. Every possible world in which we are the center of attention and every possible event revolves around our joys, sorrows, fears, desires, and insecurities. There's a pattern: every world is related to future possibilities. The future and its creation are dependent on our past.

Overall, the past and future, as well as the external world, create a dilemma that kills our present moments and the possibility of small joys or happiness within us that need to be explored. But it exists within us. Does this imply that we should reduce the external's impact on the internal in order to live in the moment—in harmony, contentment, and happiness? The goal is to eliminate the numerous possibilities we've created within ourselves, based on the image of the outside world. But that's not easy, and it cannot be accomplished in a day. For many, it takes a lifetime. But at the very least, if we can remind ourselves of this daily and focus on the smallest events—those that encompass the infinitesimally small time interval called the present or now, with few or weak expectations—it may provide us with small, momentary, and millions of packets of happiness daily, rather than once-in-a-lifetime happiness. We simply need to accept and embrace this outlook on life.

Even a four-line unrhymed expression should be treated with more reverence than a magnificent sixty-four-line rhymed poem. Isn't it unjust if we don't? This asymmetry of expectations, happiness, and importance is what society has imposed and reinforced repeatedly. It's time to change that for the longer journey called life. I once heard that acceptance is the key. True, but our ego, the result of years of high expectations and outward-dependent happiness, views acceptance as a loss—a loss of not achieving what our inner world desired: being loved by everyone, gaining enormous respect, and not being wrong in front of others. The question is, does it really matter? This is inextricably linked with other people's expectations and happiness, but who we lose in all of this is our own inner self, which remains untouched and untapped.

Acceptance is difficult. We know we must accept but find it hard to do so. Why? The reason is the cumulative fear we've developed since birth. Fear of what others will think, fear of being shunned by a group of people who don't know what they want from life. Are we doing ourselves justice—our unabashed, untapped creative freedom? The fear of taking the first step, of having our ideas and expressions rejected, prevents us from accepting our own inner craziness.

Acceptance doesn't mean the end of the world for us then and there; it means the start of an inward journey that is far more productive, creative, and full of joy and happiness. Once we understand that, we can take a step closer to realization. The creative person should at least try the first step, which has the potential to bring infinite freedom—the never-ending peace within our world of limitless creative potential.

The world within us is vast and unexplored. Although it is based on the world around us, it does not end there. It awaits our exploration. There lies the pinnacle of creativity. This world is distinct from the infinite possible worlds based on our anxieties and fears. Its uniqueness stems from the fact that it does not rely on external parameters to create happiness. It doesn't require anyone else but us. Nothing—absolutely nothing—matters there: friends, family, or any external object. It's pure, full of peace, creativity, and contentment, and most importantly, it's under our control, unlike the external, which can turn upside down in seconds. So, the moment we understand and accept our inner world—our quirks, our bit of craziness—we become acceptable to ourselves, which is extremely important and necessary to go beyond what awaits us: the creative world that wants us to arrive and take charge of everything. Therein lies the key to infinite bliss, unabashed freedom, and never-ending joy. Simply muster the courage to take the first step and discover the secrets of life, both within and without. Just go ahead and give it a try.

SPACE AND SILENCE

CHAPTER THIRTY-FOUR

IS SELFLESS LOVE AN OXYMORON?

Can we truly love someone selflessly? This is a question that keeps popping into my head. There are times in our lives when we find ourselves at a crossroads of inner egotistical squabbles—the classic devil and angel sitting on our shoulders, stretching us between what is correct and what is not, from their point of view. The devil would force the "I" to feel important, as if it were the center of the solar system, while the angel would dissolve it into the vast array of stars and galaxies. Loving someone without any expectations—or without expecting anything in return—has always been held in high regard. But does the mental state of loving someone without expecting anything in return exist? Can we, these moving frames of flesh and blood, ever reach that state? I'd rather dig deeper because these questions have repeatedly prompted me to consider the concepts of loving someone and being loved by someone. So, too, is the role of bearing the mental anguish that comes with navigating the dichotomy creators on our shoulders. I'd like to point out that the term "love" is used broadly here; I include all types of relationships, whether they are parental, romantic, or something as drastic as one-way admiration.

Consider a world in which people have no emotions. To begin with, based on our human experience, we would say that imagining such a world is nearly impossible. Or, if we did, we should stop calling them humans and instead refer to them as robots, not humanoids—and I certainly do not want to discuss a world of zombies. Also, because there are no emotions, we should not imagine predators running around. So, I believe we can easily replace the word "human" with "emotional human" without changing the internal meaning. But there is one difference: the term "emotional human" cannot be used alone; it must be used in conjunction with another term, namely the relationship between the human and its surroundings. The term "surroundings" is used broadly here, encompassing other humans, animals, and even inanimate objects. This raises another question: can emotions arise in the absence of interaction? That's something to think about another time. For now, we'll assume that emotions can only be elicited through interactions.

Returning to the term "love," it is an emotion within us that must be the result of brain chemistry, but how it affects our lives is where my interest lies. The concept of selfless, pure love is so noble that it extends to realizing something divine, godly, or free of the clutches of the material world. But then the question arises: is it even possible to achieve that mental state in which we love someone selflessly without expecting anything in return? Is selfless love, like "musical noise," an oxymoron? I'd like to examine this from two perspectives. The first is the optimistic-resilience perspective, which holds that such a state exists, and we humans can fully realize it and strive to achieve something close to it. The second is the pragmatic viewpoint, which holds that no such perfect state exists, and there is no such thing as selfless love.

I'll start with the optimistic-resilience viewpoint—the conviction that, yes, a selfless love mental state exists and can be attained. The question is: how can someone reach the point where they love the other person without expecting anything in return, without allowing their ego to interfere? It is human nature to expect something in return; good behavior demands good behavior, and this is how we survive in society. Without such reciprocity, everyone would be rude and unruly, which wouldn't bode well for peaceful, happy survival in society. Our conditioning interferes with our ability to become selfless toward any behavior, and this is reflected in our attitude toward love. Other emotional manifestations of expectations include jealousy, egotistical behavior, anger, hopelessness, low self-esteem, and more. These behaviors become more noticeable when affection or liking for someone is present.

If person A loves person B—even to the point of wanting to spend the maximum amount of time with them, enjoying their attention for life—should person A expect to receive the same attitude from person B? Even from a parent's point of view, if they take care of their children, tending to every aspect of their lives—providing them with mental, moral, and material support—shouldn't they expect their children to grow up and look after them? Isn't this self-evident? Particularly in collectivist cultures like ours. Can person A or a parent stop expecting anything in return from the other important person in their life? The optimistic viewpoint holds that selflessness can be attained through understanding one's own nature, which may lead to detachment from life's material pursuits. The simple realization that we have no control over how others feel about us may help in the development of selflessness. Loving someone does not imply that the other person must return our feelings with the same enthusiasm we have for them. Isn't it that easy? But why can't we reach that level of understanding? We cannot make someone feel the same way about us. Should we even try?

The question is: what should we do to adopt that attitude? The answer most likely lies in the mental worlds of expectations that we create. Our minds are constantly predicting the future, anticipating and assessing potential situations based on our past experiences. This should be stopped because it is the source of most of our problems. We mentally create situations that align with our expectations, as painless as possible. Our inner drive to avoid pain and increase the happiness of the other person leads us to expect the same feelings and attitudes from them. There is another aspect to this: we do not want to endure pain because, inevitably, negative and painful situations arise. In those cases, we ignore or cherry-pick only the situations that go our way.

I believe one can achieve selflessness only if they stop thinking about future possibilities, stop creating ego-satisfying mental worlds, or keep both positive and negative possibilities open and ready. One should try not to create mental worlds while also maintaining a balance between negative and positive possibilities, preparing for any situation. Although it may seem easy to say all this, it may take a lifetime to develop such an attitude. Especially when other factors, such as our self-image, self-doubt, self-respect, and desire to be loved, interfere. Undoubtedly, it's difficult, but if we develop the maturity to try, things may become easier. At first, we may experience depressive thoughts, but eventually, acceptance may come naturally. If love is true, give it wings; if it's meant to come back, it will.

The pragmatic position argues that no such selfless state exists, that "selfless love" is a misnomer, and that one should expect, control, and receive the same level of affection from the other person. The problem with this perspective is that we continue to fit everything into our mental-world expectations in order to gain the other person's attention and feelings. If they don't meet our expectations, this can lead to extremely disturbing, messy, and depressive situations. Unfortunately, this is what most people experience. This is where the majority of our problems arise. It's a precarious situation. If one is fortunate, that's great, but if not, it can lead to severe depression. At the end of the day, we can only try and cannot control the other person's feelings and attitudes toward us. This doesn't mean we should abandon all effort, but we must recognize that we cannot control the outcome. To overcome this mindset, one must let go of the concept of control.

Most of us experience both perspectives at some point in our lives. Generally, one starts as pragmatic and becomes optimistic and resilient with experience, maturity, and understanding. It is entirely up to us which path we take, as peace and happiness are what matter. Love should be constructive rather than destructive. The importance of mental and spiritual growth through love cannot be overstated, but it is not easy. It takes a great deal of endurance, understanding, experience, and maturity to overcome jealousy, insecurity, possessiveness, control, and the massive mental palace of never-ending expectations.

CHAPTER THIRTY-FIVE

THE THIRD PERSON PERSPECTIVE

The beauty of reflection and introspection resides in taking a detached view of oneself and one's surroundings. It has the potential to allow for impartial judgments and choices. Internal ideation becomes more distinct and subtle when the "I" or "my" changes into "this," even for a moment. In our daily lives, we encounter instances where it is almost impossible to seek assistance because our internal expressions are too muddled to articulate.

Our lives are made more challenging by perplexing notions and unnecessary egotism. Acceptance is thrown out the window in this very process. Then, given that these positions can lead to sadness, anxiety, and other problems, the question becomes: what exactly should be done in such situations? The best option is to consult a therapist or close friend who can understand your situation and guide you in the right direction. The second-best course of action is to look at yourself objectively.

Now that we are aware of the ideal approach, the main challenge is getting people to accept it. Our internal decision-making mechanism becomes darker as we immerse ourselves more deeply in I-ness. While thinking in the third person, you must imagine speaking to yourself from the outside. For instance, if your name is ABC, you might often wonder why things happened to you the way they did, what you ought to do next, and other similar thoughts. This could add layers related only to your concerns and doubts, complicating the difficult situation rather than offering a clear solution.

Although acceptance is one of the most basic concepts we have used throughout our lives, it is a very challenging process to go through. But why is it challenging? The answer lies in our perspective, which must be changed with a great deal of practice. Change makes it easier. The strength of this approach is found in the third-person viewpoint I'm referring to. Although being an outsider to oneself is difficult, it can be attempted.

The instant you separate your mind and body from "this" mind and body of "ABC," you remove yourself from the position of being the only one responsible for solving your own difficulties. The more objectively you can think while stepping outside of yourself, the greater your comprehension will be. You must first analyze the issue and identify its underlying causes. It can be challenging to even recognize the precise nature of the problem you are experiencing. Often, we don't understand it ourselves. You must ask "ABC": Is the issue connected to any specific people, circumstances, environments, or something else?

If this is established, the next consideration must be whether the issue originates with the individual, circumstance, or environment. Why is that even a problem? Is it causing you emotional or mental stress? Is it causing problems in your career or studies—or both? Why is it affecting you? What role are you playing in that situation? Have you encountered a situation like this before? What was the solution at that time?

The hardest part now is to figure out the solution. If you consider it from a "no-ego position," what could have been the right course of action? This is the point at which most individuals don't want to cry or continue thinking. In our daily lives, we tend to think primarily from a self-centric perspective. It's very challenging to overcome this obstacle. It's almost as though we know that material things are fleeting, but we pursue them nonetheless.

Similarly, though it's nearly impossible to avoid, even if we know what to do, accepting it is extremely difficult. The only way to handle this is to imagine you are speaking to someone named "ABC," who is actually you. The experience will be akin to conducting your own interview while acting as your own counselor. I think everyone should try it at least once in their lives because it's an enlightening process.

CHAPTER THIRTY-SIX

LOVE, WITH A PINCH OF SALT

My roommate and I were talking about love, infatuation, one-sided love, affairs, and so on the other day. We've both been through so much in our lives that we've ended up becoming unapologetic prophets of love (the term love guru is old and outdated). Before I proceed, I must introduce both of us. I, the writer of this blog, am a thirty-three-year-old man who has spent four or five years of his life thinking about love rather than his career, which is an accomplishment in and of itself. My roommate is about eight summers younger than I am and has a small but intense amount of experience living life with his heart on his sleeve.

My sleeve is torn now, so I keep my heart hidden behind a hideous cover, while my roommate still has the freedom and age to gain more experience and wisdom about the dos and don'ts of love. Our discussion covered a wide range of topics and viewpoints, but it came to a close when we summed it up in one sentence: "Love, with a pinch of salt."

Our discussion began with the question of whether one-sided love is good or bad, devastating or not, emotionally damaging or not. My stance was that it is damaging because when you are simply admiring someone from afar, expectations are bound to arise. Unfulfilled expectations are what cause emotional harm. It is also true that one should never have expectations in one-sided love or in liking someone. I should also mention that I don't want to get into the philosophical or spiritual aspects of it here.

My entire perspective on love is based on admiration and affection. So, unfulfilled expectations, desires, and efforts from oneself are what cause internal issues such as depression and loneliness. My roommate interrupted to say that it is not damaging or destructive if one is not obsessed or mad about the person of interest. Basically, I got the idea or concept of expectations and the baggage of unreciprocated feelings. But how can someone admire another person if they have no expectations?

This opens up another path: if X is admiring or loving Y and there is no reciprocation from Y, it is not Y's fault, and Y should not be blamed because one can try anything but never force someone to fall in love or admiration. It will happen if it's meant to. The issue is one of ego—if X does not receive what he or she expects from Y, it may lead to feelings of worthlessness, self-doubt, and critical self-evaluation. This is especially problematic at this point in time. It is crucial for X to keep these things in mind to avoid falling into an expectation trap in the future.

We also discussed and clarified one minor point: when love is one-sided, X will generally never see any fault in Y. Even the most egregious flaw will be easily overlooked if X is head over heels. It's a situation where one could even find peace in the fact that Y is a mass murderer. The entire focus would be on surface features, such as how the other person looks, speaks, communicates, and interacts. The qualities desired would be efficiently cherry-picked throughout. As long as there are no expectations, this is fine, but isn't hope becoming a silent killer in this situation?

When X and Y enter a relationship full of mutual love and passion, the flaws will eventually surface. They will become more visible to one another. If X no longer wants to be with Y after going through these surface flaws, it then becomes a mere attempt to rekindle kindness or, more accurately, to stretch the relationship even after the feeling of being in it has passed. This is where the problem arises—when people attempt to stretch and prolong the entire situation, leading to the slow death of the beautiful relationship.

The longer it takes, the more painful the breakup is, and the longer it takes to cope with the situation. It also takes a lot of mental energy to go through the entire process. In any case, this dispels the notion of apologetic, zero-expectation, one-sided love. Although the same could be said of a two-sided love affair, it is easier said than done in either one-sided or two-sided relationships. It's better to love someone with a grain of salt. The pinch of salt here refers to minimizing unwanted and unnecessary expectations.

Following this, another line of thought emerged in which the entire process of developing a romantic relationship was viewed in two distinct ways: top-down and bottom-up. The former occurs when the attraction is more physically oriented in the beginning, when the idea of being together starts with enjoying each other's physical aspects. So it begins on the surface and gradually moves downward toward a more spiritual and intellectual understanding of each other, until the pair reaches a level of emotional understanding that completes the relationship.

The disadvantage of the top-down approach is the involvement of human material nature. If the entire foundation of the relationship is based on physical aspects, it may take a lot of effort to reach the emotional, sentimental, and intellectual connection. As dopaminergic neurons become accustomed to the immediate gratification of the pair's physical alignment, the spiritual and intellectual components can become tedious and boring. It's the desire for instant gratification that worsens things.

Now, with the bottom-up approach, the relationship begins with understanding, based on the spiritual and intellectual connection of both parties. This has its own issues. Once the "pious objectives of love" are revealed, raising it to the level of romance and intimacy becomes a difficult task. As the pair is drawn to the intellectual phenomenon of each other, romantic and physical intimacy can make the whole experience of love seem impure and dizzy. Now the question becomes: what works?

Both the bottom-up and top-down approaches are important. The asymmetry between the two causes emotional imbalance in the relationship because one party will always try to get the emotional ball in their court, which is driven by ego. Emotional balance occurs when both individuals achieve stability, i.e., they reach the exact center of the top-down and bottom-up approaches. This requires time, effort, trust, compromise, and so on. In order to reach the level of understanding required to strengthen the foundation of a relationship and take it to the next level, one must also take ego into account.

Our discussion came to an end after we theorized love and attempted to develop a new model of the process of entering into a romantic relationship. I would also advise the reader not to take the preceding *"gyaan"* too seriously because it was simply a discussion for the sake of discussion, with no further or prior research. This was simply a case of our perspectives overlapping in some way. So, take not only love with a pinch of salt, but also this writing on the relationship process with a pinch of salt.

CHAPTER THIRTY-SEVEN

AT THE END OF THE CYCLE

Have you ever wondered why nearly everything in this universe is circular, both literally and metaphorically—or, more precisely, periodic or recurring? It's periodic, from the revolution of any planet around a star to the movement of electrons around the nucleus and the rotation of every celestial object. It's as if you trace a point on the earth, and as night turns to day and day turns to night, you'll find a beautiful circle.

The question of why everything repeats seems to have an answer in physics, but does this lead us to a mechanistic universe governed by a set of laws without the need for a creator? Another example is the birth-death cycle. Everything, from the microscopic to the cosmic to the living, goes through this. Considering the existence of the soul and the theory of karma would lead us back to this cycle.

If you look closely, you will notice that the cyclic process goes through phases. For instance, the moon's phases—from full moon to new moon and back again—pass through several meta-states. On one end, the moon shines brightly, inspiring writers and poets, while on the other, practitioners of the occult are enticed to achieve supernatural stardom. The fascinating aspect is that every full moon is followed by a new moon, and vice versa. The polar opposite appears to be the closest match. Does this imply that at the extremes of anything, the opposite occurs? Can we say the same about the human mind and behavior?

From Buddha to Osho, everyone has reflected on this: spiritualism awaits you at the pinnacle of materialism. Is it because one becomes exhausted with never-ending wants and needs? Is peace the mind's last resort? Can extreme attachment result in detachment? At the pinnacle of emotional harakiri, when the mind is doing everything it can to escape the situation, when even a sliver of hope seems to ignite the daylight for the restless and frustrated, two extreme phenomena may occur.

Either the mind breaks all the chains and quickly escapes, or it accepts the chains and leaves with them. Peace is achieved in both cases. The only difference is that in one, the chains are broken, whereas in the other, the chains are simply untangled and removed from the body itself. We can't say which is better because it varies from person to person.

A better illustration would be sand. If you squeeze it too hard, you will lose all the tiny grains. The hold represents the mental states of restlessness, attachment, and pain, while the grains represent the physical states. It's like peeling an onion; once all the layers are removed, what's left is nothing. The lull before a storm or the eerie silence after a storm, the darkest hour before dawn—there are numerous examples like these.

Our minds are strange creatures. They can take you to the heights of maxima and then topple you to the depths of minima. Extreme amounts of attachment, love, desire, need, and frustration lead to the land of nowhere—to the no-man's-land where there is nothing: no love, no desire, no need, and no attachment. But does this lead to the pinnacle of peace? Perhaps, perhaps not. It may depend on the individual's experience and realization. The greater the realization, the greater the emptiness; the greater the realization, the greater the peace.

All of these are mental states brought on by external events in one's life. These events, in turn, shape and create the internal world. When the internal world is hit by cyclonic emotions, the clouds become so dense that little sunlight reaches the layers of the mind. Those who continue to try to remove the clouds will either succeed with all due force or succumb to the suffocating stronghold of the oxygen-depleted internal atmosphere.

As previously stated, when acceptance occurs, something else can also happen. The terrifying clouds and massive storms begin to appear beautiful and magnanimous. When the frustrations and powerful attachments appear vibrant and dynamic, those clouds lose their fervor and charm. That is when the self awakens from its slumber.

It brings the mind out of hibernation and saves it by allowing it to accept the situation. This leads to detachment, and detachment leads to peace. The allure of something new fades, and the excitement fizzles out. The realization and comprehension deepen. The mind moves from the new moon to the full moon at the end of the cycle. The attachment weakens its grip, resulting in nothingness and emptiness in the individual. The mind is indeed beautiful.

97

CHAPTER THIRTY-EIGHT

SPACE AND SILENCE

In this vastness, where we are no more than a tiny dot—or even far less than we could ever imagine—full of gazillions of cosmic entities roaming around, maintaining a fine balance with the cycle of birth and death, where it appears to have nothing but is still full of mysteries to be unleashed, it is what we conscious beings look into to find a reflection of ourselves in the minute, twinkling scattered dots—the medium where the stars float around—the space. The space that gives birth to so many complexities also absorbs the tiniest details, leaving no trace of them. That space, which is also around us, allows us to move, build, design, and even destroy. Is space, however, limited to our immediate surroundings? What about here, there, and everywhere? Isn't it also in our heads? The importance of space is beyond comprehension. The space we require in a relationship is the result of our never-ending thought machine. This entire machinery of space, both outside and inside, is grounded in something much more fundamental: the one that gives rise to space, emptiness, or, as I prefer to call it, silence. The very nature of the space within and without our mortal body is tied to silence. We will never be able to separate space from silence or silence from space because they are so intricately intertwined.

Nature goes berserk before and after the storm, uprooting everything to change the dimensions of the environment. But there is something that leaves a mark both before and after: the eerie calm, the never-ending silence. Even in the midst of a massive storm, what remains is silence, always ready to expand its own enigma, its own demeanor—and that is the beauty of silence. Our lives are nothing more than manifestations of these two beautiful concepts. Our entire personalities, minds, visions, goals, and aspirations are derived from the essence of space and silence. Every spiritual being seeks the exemplary moment of quietness, the meditative state of nothingness, in order to experience the silence hidden within the headspace. Every type of meditation tries to take you from the noisy, disturbing juggling act of the past and future to the beautiful flow of the "now," the magnificent present, the heavenly abode of silence—and inside the silence lives the master, the self, the one who is nobody but you. The one who has been traveling since time immemorial, changing clothes and dreaming of breaking free from this dream, of realizing and becoming absorbed in this magnanimous, gigantic universe, nature, the never-ending, omnipresent, omniscient space.

Human societies would never have formed if there were no relationships, no interaction, and no communication. We are constantly transmitting information in every way possible—capturing, processing, understanding, and returning the signal to allow information to flow in the space around us. This never-ending give and take also requires rest in order for the complex time machine over our shoulders to function effectively and efficiently. What is required is silence, which begins with some amount of space, to rejuvenate, to instill the notion of emptiness, to give the relationship the much-needed kickstart. By "relationship," I don't just mean the one between two people, but also the one between us and anything to which we are related. It could be the necessary evil kept in your pocket—the cell phone—or the one that allows you to do anything: the thinking machine. It is sometimes necessary for all of us to separate ourselves from our own minds in order to seek eternal quietness, to remain engulfed in stillness, the starting point of silence.

We are all thirsty—thirsty to be with ourselves, which is crucial, and this can happen when we give ourselves that much-needed break. It is the same with a relationship between two people. Here, a break does not mean a dead end or a never-ending halt, but rather a period of time to rejuvenate, recalibrate our minds, and polish and shine our souls. It will be beneficial not only to the individual and his or her work but also to the relationship between the individual and their surroundings. Individuals and societies can only thrive if they understand the underlying philosophy of this ultimate arrangement. Space is that structure made of silence's bricks, held together by the glue known as nature. If you remove each brick one by one to decipher the structure of this building, all that remains is the glue that wants to be discovered by you.

From early man to sophisticated man, from the wheel to the Voyager spacecraft, the only reason for survival has been creativity. The divergent and convergent manifestations of innumerable permutations and combinations going on inside our heads have led us to devise a variety of ways to survive in this big, bad world.

The novel, original output that caused paradigm shifts is our creative output, and the process of obtaining it is what creativity is all about. Surprisingly, we can also find the concept of space and silence within it.

The creative process is like a storm, with some definitive moments of eternal silence that shape the creative product and aid in selecting the best possible solution or way out of hundreds of thousands. The creative process is full of possible combinations, but the best one appears when the creative process is disrupted, when we do something completely different. That is when silence comes into play, dutifully and meticulously selecting the best possible solution from the solution space. We take nothingness for granted, even dismissing it as useless, but it is in that zone where silence thrives, making the space better, more suitable, and increasing the relationship's longevity—whether it's the relationship between the being and itself or between the being and its surroundings.

There will be times in our lives when we go through enormous upheavals, destructive mindsets, irritating frustrations—when things won't look as good as they did before, when the road will seem all uphill, when both the destination and the journey will seem impossible. That's when we must all sit down and give ourselves a break—to provide ourselves with space that will be filled with stillness and, most importantly, silence. The same holds true for all human relationships. If you want to be together for a long time, to last forever, these are two basic pearls of wisdom you must imbibe within yourself and initiate yourself into this wonderful, mind-boggling philosophy of space and silence.

SPACE AND SILENCE

About The Author

Shuborno Chakroborty is a versatile writer and thinker with a deep passion for exploring the intersection of science, technology, philosophy, and the human experience. He has published three books: *The Lost Prophet*, a collection of poems available on Amazon KDP; *The Divine Comedy*, a compilation of short stories and microfictions published by Notion Press; and *Mythical Sunshine*, a novella published by Notion Press. Shuborno's writing reflects his multidisciplinary thought process, blending his varied interests into compelling poems and fiction that challenge readers to think beyond the ordinary.

Shuborno has an interdisciplinary academic background, holding a BSc (Honors) in Physics from the University of Delhi, a master's in Cognitive Science from the Centre of Behavioural and Cognitive Sciences, Allahabad, and a master's in Public Policy (Science, Technology, and Innovation) from the Indian Institute of Technology, New Delhi.

Currently, Shuborno is a guest faculty member at the School of Public Policy, IIT Delhi, where he teaches a refresher course on applied mathematics. In addition to his academic role, he serves as director of Inscope Social Foundation, a Section 8 company dedicated to cultivating an innovative mindset and promoting science communication at the grassroots level. He is also a freelance author and mathematics popularizer for Pearson Education, India, and has co-authored the middle school mathematics textbook *Maths-Ace Prime*. Shuborno has organized several workshops for teachers and students across the country for Pearson education. Recently, he completed a stint at the Asian University for Women in Chittagong, Bangladesh, where he taught and trained pre-college students in applications of mathematics and creative problem-solving.

Shuborno was also invited to the Naval War College in Goa for Naval Higher Command Courses (NHCC-34, 36) by the Indian Navy to lecture on leadership, creative thinking, and basic statistics to navy and army officers. He has delivered lectures for the National Institute of Open Schooling (NIOS) on topics in applied psychology.

Shuborno's unique voice and perspective continue to captivate audiences as he weaves together the mysteries of the universe, the intricacies of the human mind and behavior, and the ever-evolving landscape of society and technology.